Published and written by Phil Simeon

ISBN-13: 978-1725693913
ISBN-10: 1725693917

This book is dedicated to my children, Jane and Lenny.

Storytime is fun and you never know
where it might take you...

Once there were three young elves named Zippy, Bippy, and Toppy. They were two brothers and a sister. Oddly, they found themselves living far from their home in the North Pole. Instead of being at home they had to live in a cozy cave inside a beautiful mountain. All kinds of families went to that mountain for fun and vacations. Now it wasn't too often that elves lived in places where there were people around. Elves didn't really like being around people, especially adults who treated them like pets. If a person touched them they would lose their magical toy making powers.

But how did they find themselves living so far from their home at the North Pole? One day, when they were on their parents' sled coming home from a family trip, they fell off the sled. Their poor parents didn't know this had happened and continued on to the North Pole. So the elves had to find a cozy cave to live in, and come up with a plan to get back to the North Pole and see their parents again.

The cool thing about elves is that they would wake up at night to have some fun and do their magical work. Their favorite spot was the hotel pool. They would have a blast playing tag, sliding, and jumping in the pool.

After swimming the elves would sneak into the back of Molly's toy store in the mountain village. They would work hard to make lots of toys like doll houses, airplanes, and race cars. The elves made amazing toys they hoped kids would love. They would leave the toys they made all neatly laid out for the store owner, Molly. After a night of fun and work the elves would scurry home for a snack and a sleep.

Molly would get to the toy store early in the morning. But no matter how early she arrived, much to her surprise there were all kinds of new toys on the shelves. She had no idea who made them or who put them there. Was it magic? Could it be Santa's elves? Molly asked everyone in the village if they knew who made the toys or how the toys got there. Nobody knew.

Now Zippy, Bippy, and Toppy only had two wishes. The first was to find their way back to their parents who they missed dearly. And the second wish was to work for Santa. After all, for a toy maker, Santa's workshop was the best place to work. They shared their ideas about how to get home.

Zippy thought they could use someone's cell phone to call the North Pole. Bippy thought they should make capes and see if they could fly like superheroes. Toppy thought they should try to find a bottle with a genie in it to grant their wishes.

After talking about their ideas they were still not sure how to get back to the North Pole. So they decided it would be a great idea to build more toys while they thought about it some more.

7

The elves had no idea that the news of the amazing toys they were building had made its way to Santa. He was excited to learn that magical toys were being made outside of the North Pole. Santa knew that only elves could make toys that amazing.

He opened his magic elf book that showed all of the elves who were making toys that year. He noticed the names of 3 elves that he knew were not working in his workshop in the North Pole. They were two brothers and a sister. Their names were Zippy, Bippy, and Toppy. Santa knew they must be the ones making the mysterious and magical toys in the mountain village.

Santa remembered hearing about three elves that had been lost.
They had fallen off their parents' sled returning to the North Pole.
The parents could not find their elf children and were so upset.
Santa let the parents know right away that he knew where Zippy, Bippy, and
Toppy were living. Their parents wanted to see the elves right away.

Santa reminded them that this might not be a good idea. After all, people
might find out about the elves and try to hug them. A hug from people woul
mean the elves would lose their magical toy making powers. Santa promised
the elves' parents they would be safe. He asked them if he could be the one
to go rescue Zippy, Bippy, and Toppy. The parents agreed, as long as they
could join the rescue.

9

Santa had a great idea of how to rescue them. The Santa Claus parade was coming to the mountain village on Saturday. Santa knew that would be the best opportunity to rescue Zippy, Bippy, and Toppy.

Santa had hundreds of elves working for him on all kinds of different things. One special elf was the Elf Wizard. She had incredible powers and was the leader of the elf ninjas. She was so creative and brave. The Elf Wizard had helped rescue Santa and other elves from danger many times, so Santa knew he could rely on her. There was one time Santa was flying on his sled and he fell off. Elf Wizard instantly created a huge candy cane out of thin air. She used it to pull Santa back up to the sled in a jiffy. Santa never forgot that and talks about it all the time.

But Elf Wizard was only as good as her team of elf ninjas. These ninjas had the skills to come to the rescue in emergencies. Sometimes Santa would get stuck in chimneys after eating too many treats that kids left for him. When that happened the elf ninjas would come to the rescue. It took a lot of practice to become an elf ninja. That's why elf ninjas were so amazing at rescuing Santa and other elves in emergencies. They got to wear a cool uniform that no other elf was allowed to wear.

Santa called his Elf Wizard and ninjas into his office to talk about rescuing Zippy, Bippy, and Toppy. Santa loved talking with all of the different elves in the North Pole. They were all valuable and all had important jobs. Santa believed in elf teamwork, and he ensured that no matter what job each elf had, it was an important one to the huge elf team.

As Christmas got closer Santa talked a lot with the elves who lived on shelves in people's homes across the world. They knew everything about kids, their neighbors, and friends. That helped Santa figure out who was naughty or nice. Santa and the ninja elves came up with a rescue plan for Zippy, Bippy, and Toppy. They were all so excited to rescue their friends.

14

Back in the mountain village Zippy, Bippy, and Toppy were having so much fun making toys in Molly's workshop. They knew it was almost morning time and that Molly would be opening the store soon. They had no idea that today was the Santa Claus parade in the village, and Santa and their parents were arriving soon.

Time was running out for the elves. They really needed to get out of the store and back to their cave safely. It was daylight now and that meant people would wake up and start walking around. It was now or never they had to go. Just as they were about to leave they saw a dad walk by the store. Luckily, he didn't see the elves in the store.

16

The elves immediately dropped what they were doing and scurried to the back of Molly's store. They took a peek out the back door and did not see any people. A family walked by with two young kids. They were talking about the amazing toys found in Molly's toy store and wondering who made them.

The elves peeked out of the bush and no one was there. They hurried down the path and heard more people. They jumped into the next bush and hid behind the garbage can. The people walking by them threw their empty coffee cups towards the garbage. One missed and landed right on Bippy's hat. Bippy was not happy about that. While taking the cup off Bippy's hat Toppy could not stop laughing.

The laughing had to stop because the hardest part of getting back to the cave was coming up. The elves had to get across the main village road without being seen or touched.

While they were hiding they noticed the main street was set up differently. It looked like Christmas time! There was a sign that said "Santa Claus Parade Today." The elves couldn't believe the parade had arrived. They were so excited that Santa was coming to town they started jumping up and down. Then they realized they were making too much noise and someone might see them.

While all of this was happening Zippy, Bippy, and Toppy had no idea the elf ninjas had landed in the mountain village early in the morning. They had travelled there on Santa's sled for the big rescue.

The elf siblings still had not made it back to their cave. They were feeling trapped and more and more people were gathering on the street. All of a sudden, a little girl walking with her parents noticed the elves. Toppy looked and winked at the girl and signaled with her finger to be quiet. Toppy whispered to the girl that she was on Santa's 'nice' list. The little girl smiled and couldn't believe the great news. She really wanted to give Toppy a big hug.

It was now or never for the elves. They had to get across the main street.
Just as they took their first steps to the other side, the elf ninjas swooped
in out of the sky and took Zippy, Bippy, and Toppy by surprise.
The elf ninjas flew everyone through an open window into a gingerbread
house that only elves could fit in. It was a big surprise and at first the elves
had no idea what had just happened. But to their relief, they realized it
was an amazing rescue by the elf ninjas.

They had managed to get into the gingerbread house safely. They all gave each other hugs, and the elf ninjas told Zippy, Bippy, and Toppy not to worry. The great news was that their parents and Santa were very close by. The challenge for the elf ninjas was somehow getting everyone into Santa's sled.

The next part of the ninjas' rescue plan was to jump on Santa's parade float as it passed the gingerbread house. Zippy had a sack of toys with him that the elves had made. He wanted to bring them with him. The other elves tried to convince him to leave them in the gingerbread house. He didn't want to. He wanted to show Santa and his parents the work the elves had done so that they could work in the North Pole. Being good teammates, the elf ninjas understood that the toys would be coming with them. It was going to make the escape to Santa's float a little more daring.

The float was approaching and the plan was to scurry out as quickly as possible and jump onto the float. They really had to avoid people as they ran to Santa's float. The elf ninjas didn't realize that the Elf Wizard was on the float. She was amazing at creating things out of thin air.

As the float got close to the gingerbread home the Elf Wizard cast a candy cane bridge from her hand onto the home. The elves hopped on one by one and skipped across onto Santa's float. Zippy was last and people could see his toys floating out of his sack and into the air.

All of the people at the parade looked up and could not believe their eyes – was this really happening? There were elves happily skipping across a magical candy cane bridge onto Santa's float. The toys floating out of Zippy's sack looked exactly like the ones in Molly's store.

Everyone at the parade was surprised and so excited. The people ran to get a closer look at the elves and the toys floating out of Zippy's sack. But it was too late, Santa had his sled moving faster and safely taking off into the air back to the North Pole.

Zippy, Bippy, and Toppy hugged their parents for a long time. After the hugs were finished, Santa waved them over.

Santa thanked the elves for all of their hard work making amazing toys. In his hand he had 3 badges. They were the elf super toy maker badges that only the most hard working elves could get.

All of the elves' wishes had come true.

The End.

Made in the USA
Columbia, SC
18 November 2018

35025161R00020